ABRAXUS TASKER COLLEGE
JUNIOR YEAR

I0583822

ATHLETICS

AbraXus Tasker College
JuniorYear

ATHLETICS

Ali Whippe

4 Horsemen
Publications, Inc.

DEDICATION

FOR ALL THE BOYS ON THE TEAM

*B*ree Johnson stands outside the glass door of the Tutoring Center, lips pursed as she contemplates the darkness within. She checks her watch: 6:48pm. She re-reads the posted hours on the door: Mon-Thurs 10am-8pm; Fri-Sat 10am-4pm; Sun Closed.

She leans into the glass, cupping her hands around her eyes to peer in, but she can see nothing beyond the light glow of some computer monitors. The overhead lights are off, and no one moves within.

"Dammit!" she curses. "Isn't it Wednesday?" She looks down at her watch again, tapping the button on the side so it switches from the time to the date.

"Wait—why is it closed?" a voice says from behind her. "I thought they were open until 8 tonight."

"Me too," Bree commiserates, turning to face the new-comer—and all thoughts of studying flee her mind. He is big, like football player big, with broad shoulders and thick legs, a shock of brown hair framing an open, easygoing expression. "Isn't it Wednesday?" she squeaks, trying to ignore the flush of desire that pools in her middle. She has always been a sucker for the boys on the team back home.

"I thought so," he says, scanning the hours as she had done. He steps around her, careful of his size, moving slowly like one who is accustomed to the world being too small for him. He leans in as she had, cupping one hand around his eyes to see through the dark glass, then shrugs. "Maybe Miss Chapman got sick?"

Bree lifts her shoulders in return. "I guess, but she could have put up a note or something." She turns away, thoughts of studying and the test on Friday swamping her brain again. "Fuck," she curses. "I really needed someone to run through flashcards with me."

"Flashcards?" the guy repeats. "You need like a study partner?"

She turns back to look at him, taking in the XTC Stallion t-shirt tight across his chest, the simple black gym shorts ending at his knees, the white tube socks and black Adidas slides. "I don't know," she replies. "What do you know about A&P?"

He cocks his head, "Depends. You mean 'A&P,' the short story by John Updike or A&P like Anatomy and Physiology, the class?"

She stares at him, shock obvious on her face. She didn't expect him to be built like that and actually smart. There is a good chance he is smarter than she is! She took Comp 2 the previous year, so she remembers the short story. "I remember the girls in bathing suits from 'A&P,'" she offers. "How could I forget?"

"Why? You like girls in bathing suits?"

She smirks. "Duh. Who doesn't?" She smiles warmly at him. "But I remember because I had the hottest professor who read it out loud to us in class. He had the best voice," she adds.

The guy nods. "It's a good story, but you're not here to write a paper tonight, are you?"

Bree shakes her head. "No, I have an A&P test on Friday, like the class about the body." She looks down at the floor, suddenly wishing she is wearing something cuter than her pink sweatpants and white tank top, though the black bra showing through is a nice touch she hopes he appreciates.

He nods in understanding, "I took that last semester. It would have been brutal if Coach hadn't made us study constantly. I don't think I'll ever forget about the integumentary system." He raises an eyebrow at her suggestively. "I kept forgetting what it was, and Coach made me run laps until I could remember." He chuckles. "Very long night." He pauses, then adds, "Very effective."

Bree gives him a confused look. "Integu-what?"

"Integumentary," he says again, the word rolling off his tongue. "You know," he says, reaching out to touch her hand. "Skin."

"Oh," she breathes, letting him hold her hand for a long moment. "Right." She stares at him, brain trying to focus on anything, and then she blurts, "What are you here for?"

He shrugs. "I wanted to pick up a review sheet that Vince left for me," he says, "but I guess I can get it tomorrow. Not like I'm going to work on chemistry tonight anyway. I just wanted to have it for later."

"Vince?" she asks. "Is that your friend?"

"One of the guys on the team," he tells her. "He's the wide receiver."

"Is that an innuendo for something?" she asks, hoping he isn't gay. She doesn't think so, but it's always better to ask. She takes in that big body again, hope blooming in her belly. Maybe she can get something out of tonight after all.

He chuckles. "Oh no," he says, flashing her a charming smile. "Vince is as hetero as they come. Me too, though I can admit when a man is handsome as fuck."

Bree smiles back at him, very aware of his hand on hers. "I also enjoy handsome men," she says, an offer in her voice, but then she remembers her test, and other thoughts leave her mind. Her shoulders slump. "What am I going to do about that stupid test? I'm so screwed."

"Well, I could help, if you wanted," he offers.

"Really?" she asks, excitement and something else building in her chest. "With the test or the screwing?" The words spill out, and she blushes.

"Both, if you like," he offers.

"But you hardly know me," she objects. It isn't the first time she hooked up with someone she just met, but she doesn't want him to know that right away.

"No, but I'd like to get to know you." He reaches out his other hand as if to shake. "I'm Josh, cornerback for the XTC Stallions."

Bree nods like she knows what that means. She has spent a fair amount of time listening to football players talk about the sport, but she has spent most of it admiring their bodies, so position names never really matter much. She thinks he is probably a defensive player, judging by his size, and probably does something about guarding the corners of the field. She shakes his offered hand, her other still holding him, "I'm Bree, A&P noob and football fan."

"Tell you what," he suggests, leaning in, "I can help you with those flashcards."

"Really?" she asks, this time her voice skeptical. "I have a feeling we might get distracted. And I really can't fuck this one up."

He nods, face open and sincere, though flirtatious as well. "I solemnly swear I will help you learn those flashcards tonight. Scout's honor." He holds up his fingers like a Boy Scout. "What part are you on?"

"The skeleton," she groans. "I have to label all of the bones."

He nods, lifting up both of her hands, fingers pressing on the tips of hers, "Phalanges," he identifies, then slides his fingers up a little, "Metatarsals." He reaches her palm, gently squeezing the bones there, "Tarsals."

"You do know your anatomy," Bree breathes, turned on and hopeful at the same time.

"You'd be surprised," Josh says, tugging her hand to lead her away from the dark doorway. "Come back to my dorm, and I'll show you all of the bones."

Bree smiles at him. Maybe this actually can work. Nothing says she can't have sex and study tonight. Suddenly, A&P seems a lot more interesting.

osh opens the door to his dorm and gestures for Bree to enter. She isn't quite sure what to expect—is he a sloppy guy with clothes everywhere or a tidy guy with everything perfectly in place? She is glad to see that he is somewhere in between. The room is clean enough, but the blanket on the bed against the right wall is rumpled at the foot, the desk covered with several piles of papers. The other desk also has piles, but they seem neater, and the bed only has a plain white sheet on it, no blanket or pillows. There are several pairs of shoes next to the door—a mix of slides and sneakers. Far more shoes than Bree thinks Josh should have it if he lives here alone. She glances to her right, seeing the open doorway into a small interior hallway with what looks like a door to the bathroom on the left and another room like this one on the far side.

"You live here alone or with roommates?" she asks, turning to face him as he enters behind her.

"It's a quad," he tells her, "but there's only three of us in here right now. Tony just went home—he broke his leg at the game two weeks ago." He looks at her, tapping his thigh, "The femur, actually."

"I do know that one," she replies with a grin. As she watches, he grabs a sock from the top of the dresser next to the door, and in a smooth motion, hooks it on the outside of the door before shutting it. "Subtle," she tells him with a grin. "Why don't you just lock the door?"

He flips the lock and turns to her, "Because I still have two idiot roommates who don't always take a hint," he admits.

"Do they often walk in on you when you are occupied?"

He nods, "They walk in this way all the time." He gestures at the shoes piled next to the door. "They have their own entrance, but they put an entertainment center in front of it so they can play Madden on a big screen."

"And you don't mind?" she asks, taking the few steps across the room to sit on the empty bed.

He shrugs. "It's a pretty nice TV," he admits, "and I love Madden. Small price to pay to share my doorway."

"Except when you bring a girl back to your room," she observes.

He smiles, walking over and sitting on his bed across from her. "It's not like this happens all the time," he tells her. "Besides, this is an official study session."

"Of course," Bree agrees, setting her bag down on the floor next to her and taking off her flip flops. She tucks her feet up so she sits cross legged. "Totally official."

"So," he says, leaning back and crossing his feet at the ankles, shirt tightening to show off his muscled arms, "let's see those flashcards."

Bree leans down to get them from her bag, moving slowly, deliberately flashing her cleavage as she does so. When she leans back up, his eyes move from her black bra back up to her face and then down to the stack of pink index cards she now holds. She frowns, sexy time on hold as she remembers the test again. "So how do you want to do this?"

He reaches out, long arms easily crossing the space between

the beds, and she hands him the cards. "How about we make it a game?" he suggests.

"What kind of game?" she asks, turning her body to face him, wishing he would move closer to her.

"The kind where I ask you a question, and if you get it right, you get a prize, but if you get it wrong, you get a punishment."

"I'm interested," she says, "but what is a prize and what is a punishment?"

"What do you want it to be?" he asks, leaning on his knees so his upper body is closer to hers. She scoots forward on the bed so her legs hang off the edge, her feet nearly touching his. "What would be a prize for you, Bree? What do you want?" His voice has gone low, sexy.

"I want you," she says immediately.

"How do you want me?" he encourages, voice a low thrum that sends shivers up her spine.

Bree looks up at him, eyes tracing from his handsome face down that neck to those gorgeous shoulders. "I want you naked," she says boldly.

"Okay," he agrees," so that's your first prize. Now what about punishment? What do you not want?" he asks.

"I don't want you to murder me since I'm now alone in your room and I hardly know you," she blurts out.

He snorts, leaning back. "I don't plan to do anything of the sort," he promises.

"Just what a murderer would say," she quips.

"Scout's honor," he swears, lifting his three fingers in her direction. "I much prefer you alive. Maybe punishment is the wrong word though..."

Bree frowns at him. "Why don't we just figure it out as we go along?" she suggests.

He smiles in agreement, turning to the flashcards in his hands. "Ready?" Bree nods, and he holds up the card. "Tarsals," he announces.

Bree lifts up her foot, stretching out her shapely leg, and wiggles her toes.

"Nicely done," he says. "I guess that means a prize." He leans down and removes one of his socks.

She smirks at him. "Next."

He flips the card. "Patella."

She points to her kneecap. He tugs off his other sock and turns over the next card. "Ulna."

She lifts her arm and points to the bone on the inside of her lower arm. He nods, stands up, and pulls off his shirt in one smooth motion. Bree gapes at the lines of his muscles, his athlete's body making her mouth water. She reaches out as if to touch him, but he sits back down just out of her reach and picks up the stack of cards. "Clavicle."

Bree reaches up and traces the line of her shoulder, pushing her black bra strap down as she does so along with the strap of her white tank top.

"I don't know," he says. "That's also your humerus."

"Totally counts," she assures him. "Take off your pants."

He smiles, stands up, and slides his shorts off in one smooth motion. He is not wearing anything underneath them, and Bree is rewarded with a large cock level with her face. "I seem to be naked," he observes. "Renegotiation time."

"I'm totally going to suck that cock," she promises him. "I just need to get one more right."

He nods, reaching behind him for the pile of cards, flipping the top one over. "Fibula."

Bree taps the inside of her lower leg and slides off the bed onto her knees, crawling across the small space to take him in her hands, but he steps back and sits down on the bed again. "Oh no," he moans. "That's not right."

Bree sits back on her heels and looks up at him from where

she sits on the floor, unable to take her eyes off his cock. "What?"

"Fibula," he repeats, then taps the outer bone of his lower leg. He touches the inner bone, "Tibia."

"So what?" she breathes, sitting up on her knees and reaching for him.

"So that means it's time for a punishment." He stands up, reaching down to grab her hands, and lifts her easily to her feet. "Whatever shall I do with you?" he muses, spinning her around so her back is to him, his cock hard against her back. He holds her arms up over her head with one hand and lets his other slide down her arm and back to rest against her backside. "I think you might need more motivation," he says, whispering in her ear as he half turns her, pressing her side and hip against his chest. He moves his hand in a quick motion and slaps her ass.

"Oh!"

His hand is back again, cupping her ass where he just hit and squeezing. "Too much?" he asks, trailing a soft kiss along her neck.

"Oh no," Bree sighs. "I deserved that." She spins to look at him, keeping one hand up over her head and resting the other against his shoulder. He gently lifts her hand off him.

"Not yet," he tells her, releasing her other hand. "You have to get more right answers."

"You are an awful study partner," she accuses him, blowing out a breath and stepping back. "Fine. Next."

"I am a wonderful study partner," he chuckles, reaching behind him for the stack of cards again. "Maxilla."

She grins, a finger sliding up her body to rest against her upper lip. "I think I deserve a prize," she announces at his nod, and she steps forward again, eager hands reaching out to hold him. His cock is hard and smooth, and she wants more. She reaches up her other hand to touch his face, running a finger along his upper lip. "Maxilla," she repeats, and tugs him down to kiss her. His mouth is warm, lips soft as he opens them, tongue pressing against hers in a gentle rhythm to match the one she uses on his cock.

Josh breaks the kiss after a long moment, his cock hard with a small bead of wetness at the tip. He spins her around and pushes her down on his bed behind them, lifting her easily into place and settling himself on his knees between her legs. "I think you are ready for more intense studying," he tells her, sliding his hands beneath her tank top to stroke the smooth skin of her belly. Bree leans back into his pillow, moaning a little when his fingers find her nipple over her bra. She reaches around to take it off, but he grabs her hand and presses it above her head. "Oh no," he tells her. "Not yet." He traces a finger down between her breasts. "Identify this bone," he whispers.

Bree racks her brain for a moment, and then the word comes to her. "Sternum," she replies, and he smiles at her, pushing her tank top up and freeing her breasts from her bra. He brushes her nipples with his fingers, and pauses right above her, warm breath teasing her skin.

His hand trails along the side of her body, finding the bottom bone of her ribcage. "And this one?"

"12th rib," she answers, and he sucks one nipple, his right hand rubbing the other, his left still pinning her arms over her head.

Bree moans, sensation flooding her. She lifts her legs to wrap around him, trying to pull him closer, but he gently pulls away. "No," he chides, "you still have some studying to do!" He sits back, leaning on his knees, and looks down at her, studying her body, then says, "You're definitely wearing too many clothes for this." He slides the tank top over her head, and unclips her bra with skill that speaks of serious practice. Bree watches him slide her sweatpants down her hips, delighted to see his eyes light up when he sees her simple white panties.

"Very nice," he observes, tossing her pants behind him to land on the floor in front of the door. He bends down to kiss her nipple again, this time focusing on the right and then the left with the gentle pressure of his mouth. Bree slides her hands down from where he has left them above her head and wraps them around his head, pressing him to her chest.

"Yes," she tells him. "Suck it like that!" He obeys for another long moment, then pulls away, sliding down her body so his face hovers above her belly button.

"You want more?" he asks, trailing a line of kisses down from her lower belly to the top of her panties.

"Oh yes," she moans. "Much more."

His hand moves down to her foot and starts a slow run back up her leg, and he softly sings, "The foot bone's connected to the leg bone...the leg bone's connected to the hip bone.."

Bree giggles. "If only it was that easy! I wouldn't need to study anything."

"Let's see..." he says, trailing his hand around her hip. "What's this?"

Bree racks her brain. She knows this one—but she is distracted by his hands on her skin, his face so close to her. "Ilium!" The word bursts from her, and Josh smiles, sliding her panties off and kneeling between her legs. He kisses her gently directly on the clit, warm breath sending pleasure zinging through her, then looks up at her, judging her reaction. His tongue reaches out to press hard against her body just above her clit. "And this?" he breathes, watching her face closely over the hills and valleys of her body.

"Pubis," she moans and is rewarded by his tongue, warm and wet against her skin. His hand moves along her inner thigh, fingers pressing inside her in a slow maddening rhythm to match his tongue.

"You've been so good," he tells her, breath warm on her

sensitive skin, fingers continuing to move. "I think you've earned another reward."

"Please," she moans, lifting her hips to his face, and he licks her again, his tongue not wasting any time in finding the perfect spot and staying there, his fingers and mouth bringing her to the edge of an orgasm and right over it in moments. She trembles against him, all thought of bones fleeing her mind until she is entirely made of sensation. "Yes!"

He seems to forget himself then, sliding up her body to place the head of his cock against her. "You want me?" he asks, leaning down to kiss her neck and up to her chin. "You want me inside of you?"

Bree grabs his ass with both hands and pulls him closer, the echoes of the orgasm still radiating in her core, and wraps her legs around his hips. "Fuck me," she orders. "Now!"

Josh obeys, sheathing himself in one swift motion, and Bree shudders against him, hands splayed flat on his ass. "Yes!" she cries. He moves fast for a few strokes, hard and sure, and Bree clutches him hard again as the orgasm sweeps over her. He pauses, letting the moment shatter her, and he shifts, sitting up and lifting her so she sits on his lap, legs wrapped around what Bree notes are more like 12-pack abs. She moves her hands to his shoulders, using him to brace herself as she moves on him, setting the pace to her liking. She is about to come again, enjoying this new position, when he puts both hands on her hips, holding her steady and slides them around and down to cup her ass. "And this?" he asks, moving his head down to kiss her neck and shoulder.

"Uh..." Bree said, focusing on the building need in her center. "My..." She lets the word hang in the air, only needing a few more strokes to get there, and when he moves his hands back to her hips to stop her, she has just reached the edge, and sits still on him, body tightening reflexively as pleasure shoots through her again. After a moment, she looks at him with clear eyes, "What... What were you asking?"

He smirks at her, "Greedy girl!" He stands up, lifting her easily, then spins around and presses her back to the bed. He begins pumping into her hard, responding to the way she moans, the way her body curls around his.

"Yes!" she cries. "More!"

Just as she is about to come again, he pulls out of her completely and pauses. Bree tries to push herself closer, to get that cock back inside of her, but he holds her in place easily. She likes how strong he is, though at the moment, it is a little frustrating. She pouts at him.

"No," he tells her. "Not until you get it all right." His hand slides underneath her ass again, squeezing tight. "What's this called?"

"Ischium," she tells him proudly, the word floating into her mind, and presses forward again. "Now give me that cock."

Josh obliges her, "You definitely earned it!" He lets himself go, pounding into her with furious strokes, he nails digging into his back and her cries muffled against his neck, and he kisses her hard, claiming her mouth, and she comes again, and so does he, and he moves a few more times to enjoy the moment, and pauses, body pressed on top of hers, breathing heavily, hear pounding against her chest.

"Wow," Bree breathes, slowly catching her breath. "We should totally study together more often."

Josh chuckles, then slides to the side so he can rest next to her. "I expect you tomorrow night for chemistry review," he says.

"I'm not very good at chemistry," Bree tells him.

"I don't think we have to worry about chemistry," Josh says, leaning over to give her a long, slow kiss. "Besides, I have flashcards."

ree walks through the sliding doors into the XTC Stallions Sports Facility and takes a moment to marvel at the newness of the building. Most of her classes are in the Science and Humanities buildings, leftovers from the 70s obsession with block construction, but the Sports Facility is brand new and shiny with amenities. Bree reminds herself not to call it the gym, recalling Josh and the twins' faces when she said she'd meet them at the gym for midterm review.

"It's not a gym, Bree," Ryan told her. "It *has* a gym."

"Must be nice," she retorted. "The rest of us little people just have to settle for old showers in the dorms and no windows in the hallways. You guys get all the perks."

"It's not all guys," Bryan commented.

Standing in the lobby, Bree understands what they have been trying to tell her. To her right is a doorway painted with the Stallion logo, a horse in purple and silver. To the left is another door that clearly leads to a pool. Bree can smell the faint aroma of chlorine from where she stands. Maybe after the study session tonight she can get in a swim.

She turns to her right and opens the Stallions door. She is in a big hallway with many doors on both sides. She can see a state-of-the-art gym on one side with fancy weight-lifting machines and high tech treadmills. On the other side is what she assumes is a locker room, but when she walks inside, she is even more impressed. This is the cleanest locker room she's ever seen, more like the facilities for professional sports teams she's seen on TV than the high school locker rooms Bree has been in. She can hear showers running toward the back right corner of the space, and she can feel the steam in the air, so she assumes practice has finished and Josh and the boys will be ready for her soon.

There are actual lockers lining the wall to the left with two long wooden benches in front of them, and on the right is a wider bench against the wall that turns at the corner and continues along the far wall. In the corner sits the huge mascot costume, the body of the purple and silver stallion sagging back into the corner and the head resting separately on the bench beside it. Along the outside of the shower wall are two large steel bathtubs, one clearly steaming with hot water, and the other filled but not hot. A few large low to the ground massage tables fill the rest of the space along the back wall. There is another hallway in the back corner, and Bree assumes it leads to the practice field behind the building, and probably the coach's office.

Bree wanders over to the hot tub, letting her fingers dip into the water.

"Nice," she mumbles, wishing she could climb in. She assumes the players use it to soothe their aching muscles. "Must be nice."

"It is nice," Bryan says, the tall defenseman walking out of the showers to find her standing by the tub. He wears a white towel wrapped around his hips, the cloth setting off the dark tone of his skin. Bree takes in the muscles of his chest, something she has seen while in Josh's room occasionally, but never so close. He really is a beautiful man.

"What's nice?" Ryan asks, walking in. A mirror image of his brother, the two boys standing next to one another is enough to get Bree's imagination going. She has had a few more "study" sessions with Josh, but she has never played with his roommates. Seeing them bare chested in this light makes her rethink her decisions this semester.

"The tub," Bryan tells him.

'You should get in," a third voice joins them, Josh walking in with a towel as well.

Bree gives them a skeptical look. "Right now? But there's people in here."

Josh shrugs. "It's just us." He looks at the twins. "We had to do a few more drills before Coach was satisfied tonight."

Something in the way he says it makes Bree wonder what Coach Smith considers satisfaction, but the thought flees as she stares at the three beautifully-sculpted bodies before her. "Damn." The word escapes her before she can help it, and then she continues boldly. "I don't need my study guide," she admits. "I can just label the muscles on all of you!"

Josh grins, he and the twins exchange a look, and he raises an eyebrow at her. "You up for some rewards tonight?"

Bree meets his gaze fully. "What kind of rewards?"

"That depends on how well you can identify the muscles," he replies, glancing at the twins. "You guys in?"

"That depends on Bree," Bryan says, giving her a look that melts her stomach. "You want us to get in?"

She smiles invitingly, looking from Bryan to Ryan and back again, imagination running wild. The twins are beautiful men, and the idea of sex with all three of the players has her instantly wet. "Three is always better than one," she comments. She glances behind her at the still steaming tub. "What did you have in mind?"

Josh gestures at it. "You should get in," he tells her again.

"What if someone comes in?" she asks, looking around at the empty room. The sound of the showers has stopped, and she can't hear anyone else moving around.

Ryan shakes his head. "No one is coming in here. Everyone is at House of Beer for 2-for-1 Thursdays." Bryan nods his agreement. "We would have joined them, but I think this is more important."

"Thanks, Bryan," Bree says sweetly. "I'm glad you find my academic success so important."

"Anything for a lovely lady." He grins, then moves closer, towel swishing along his hips. "After all," he brags, "you may need someone to model certain muscles for you." He runs a hand down his glorious abs, highlighting that line that runs down to a V beneath the towel. "You can see I am well equipped for the job."

Bree swallows hard, wanting to touch him, to see just how well-equipped he is. He is so close to her now. She looks at Josh, wondering if he will mind, but he smiles at her and nods encouragingly. "Big words," she says, reaching out to touch the hard mass of his abs. "But are you a big man to match?"

Bryan's face is smug as he stands there, letting her run her hands up and down his smooth skin. "I think you will find me up to the job," he promises.

Bree's hands wander lower, finding the edge of the towel, ready to tug it loose, but she looks around first. "What about your coach?" she asks.

"Coach won't come in here," Ryan says, stepping forward to stand next to his brother. "We're all alone."

Bree looks behind them to Josh, who seems to read her mind and walks up on Bryan's other side. She looks at the beautifully-sculpted male bodies around her and grins broadly. "So," she says, "how do we begin?"

"How about we start with some muscle identification?" Josh suggests, gently taking her hand and placing it on the outside of his upper arm.

"Bicep," Bree tells him, and Josh nods, lifting her hand away and passing it to Bryan, who places it on his side, just above the towel.

"Abdominal external oblique," Bree says proudly. She is a fan of hips, so she knows that one.

Bryan grins at her. "You seem thoroughly familiar with those," he comments, taking her hand and passing it to his brother.

Ryan drags her hand along his side, then settles it on his belly button. "Rectus abodminis," she whispers. "Guys, I know all these. Abs are my favorite thing."

"Your favorite?" Ryan asks, then gently pushes her hand down over the towel to press against the sizable bulge there. "Really?"

Bree moves her hand down and quickly slips beneath the towel, reaching up to grasp Ryan's huge hard cock. "I'm also a fan of other parts," she says, slowly stroking him.

"Hey now," Bryan says. "My brother and I do everything together." He reaches for her other hand, pressing it to his own bulge, and she snakes her hand beneath his towel, gripping his matching cock and slowly stroking both of them in tandem. After a moment, she glances at Josh on her left.

"What about you?" she asks. "My hands seem to be full."

Josh reaches out to wrap his hands around her waist and lowers her gently to her knees. "I think I can find a place to fit in," he says, lifting his towel up and presenting his own erect cock at the level of her mouth.

"Always room for one more," she agrees, then takes him in her mouth, not breaking the pace of her strokes on the twins' cocks. She sucks for a long moment, and then Josh gently pulls back, not wanting to come too quickly.

"I think you've earned a reward," Ryan says.

"Let us pleasure you," Bryan echoes, and both guys lift her off her knees. Ryan tugs off her tank top as Bryan slides her sweatpants off, revealing her lacy blue bra and matching thong.

"Lovely," Josh breathes. He steps behind her, totally naked, and lifts her easily. Bryan and Ryan each take one of her feet and begin rubbing them with sure hands. Bree can feel Josh's hard cock pressing against her ass, but he holds her steady, not moving at all, letting her focus on the twins' movement instead. Slowly, they move from her feet to her calves and then to her thighs.

They move to stand on opposite sides of her legs, both sliding practiced fingers down her belly and over her thong, now wet with her excitement. "Lift her up," Ryan tells Josh, who obliges, easily hefting her to shoulder height. Bryan steps between her legs, placing one thigh on each shoulder, and moves close, burying his face between her legs. He slides her thong aside easily, tongue swiping across her sensitive skin in one long, luscious motion. Bree shudders against him. Bryan continues to lick her clit as he moves one hand up to slide gently inside her, moving slowly in and out. Bree is about to cry out, but then Ryan is next to her face, and he reaches down to kiss her, one hand tangling in her hair, and the other squeezing a nipple. Ryan's tongue is no less skilled than his brother's, and the two move in tandem. Bree puts one hand against the side of Ryan's face, holding him close to her, and lets the other wander above her head, finding Josh's face. Josh takes her fingers into his mouth, sucking eagerly.

Bree loses herself in the moment, the streaks of pleasure from between her legs, the joy of Ryan's tongue in her mouth, the feeling of weightlessness as Josh holds her aloft, and the orgasm floods her. She shakes against Bryan's face, not aware of much until she feels strong hands sliding her thong down her legs, and more hands unclipping her bra.

Then she is being lowered into warm water, the steaming heat soothing her muscles, and she sinks into pleasure. A hand finds her skin, sliding down her belly to rub her clit in slow generous circles, and she shudders against it again, the pleasure slow and sweet.

After a moment, she opens her eyes and smiles at the three naked men surrounding the tub. Bryan is to her right, so she sits up in the tub, reaches out for his cock and tugs him toward her mouth. He is big, but she can manage his length for short bursts. She sucks for a long time, then releases him, turning to face the others. She kneels at the end of the tub, gesturing for them to stand in front of her and one on each side.

Ryan takes his place at the head of the tub, the only one who she has not sucked yet, and Bryan and Josh stand on either side. She takes both cocks in her hands, slowly stroking them, and leans forward to take Ryan in her mouth. There is a long moment of sucking and stroking, and then Ryan pulls out of her grasp, visibly calming himself.

She leans back, biting her lip and looking around at all three of them. "I'm going to need some of these cocks inside of me," she announces. "Who's first?"

"Oh no," Josh says, gently removing her hand from his cock. "You have to study, remember?" He gestures at the line of muscle that forms a V shape down to his cock. "What's this called?"

"Magical?" Bree asks, leaning forward to trace the line with her tongue. Bryan takes the opportunity to swat her butt. She yelps, sinking back down into the warm water.

"You're magical," Bryan says. "What's it called?"

Bree racks her memory. "Pec-something?" she tries, looking sheepish.

"Nope," Ryan says, leaning down and scoops her out of the tub with one quick motion. She sinks dripping against his chest for a glorious moment, but he moves swiftly across the space.

Bree realizes what he is going to do about a second before he drops her into the other tub of water, which Bree notes with a shriek, is ice cold. She splutters, standing up immediately, and jumping out of it. She stands there shivering, watching all three naked men approach. Her eyes move from cock to cock to cock, and she licks her lips.

"I think she wants us, boys," Josh comments.

"But she got it wrong," Bryan says.

"She needs to earn another reward," Ryan echoes.

She looks at the line in question on all three men. "I don't know what it's called," she admits. "But I love it so much!"

"It's called the Adonis Belt," Ryan tells her.

"Or Apollo's Belt," Bryan adds.

"Although your teacher would probably label it as an iliac furrow," Josh supplies helpfully. "And it's not technically a muscle. It's a ligament."

"Cheaters!" Bree accuses. "Ligaments aren't on the midterm."

"I think ligaments might come up tonight," Ryan says, idly stroking himself as he looks at her glistening naked body.

"That's not all that will come up," Bree says, and crooks her finger at Ryan. "Come here, Big Boy. I need to feel that cock inside me."

Ryan steps over to her and lifts her up. She wraps her legs around his waist, gripping his shoulders as she settles herself on his cock. "Yes!" she moans, sinking onto him, his length filling her. He bounces her up and down a few times, holding her easily, his body stroking her clit with each motion, and she comes again, pressing her breasts to his chest as she gasps his name. When she opens her eyes again, he looks down at her in his arms.

"You want more?"

"Oh yes," she says, and then she feels Bryan settling himself against her back.

"How much more?" he whispers against her neck, the tip of his cock pressing against her ass.

"A lot more," she tells them, "but I need more action first."

"Of course," Bryan agrees, lifting her off of his brother, and sets her feet gently on the ground. "How about something more traditional then?" He gestures to the low massage table in the back of the room, and the four of them walk over to it.

"Where do you want me?" Bree asks, crawling on to the leather-covered table on her hands and knees. The padded top barely sinks beneath her weight, the table built to hold two people side-by-side.

"Right there will do," Bryan says, moving up behind her, hard cock sliding inside of her with ease. Bree gasps, and then Ryan kneels in front of her, his cock wet with her juices in front of her mouth. She reaches for it eagerly, taking him deep in her mouth as Bryan begins to fuck her harder from behind.

Josh climbs up on the bed next to her, and just as she is about to come again, he runs his hands down her back and across her ass, one finger circling her asshole and slipping inside. She grunts at the unexpected sensation, and redoubles her efforts, pumping hard against Bryan and sucking Ryan. Another wave of pleasure builds up from her center, and then Josh has two fingers inside of her ass, and she groans her orgasm, body bucking wildly.

Bryan grabs her hips and holds her steady, clearly on the edge himself, but he pulls out. He turns around, sitting on the edge of the table with his feet resting firmly on the floor in front of him, the low table making his thighs angle up to his knees. He tugs Bree close. "Climb aboard," he tells her, and she does, sliding down the incline of his legs and lifting herself on his cock again. She presses her feet into the top of the table, finally gaining the leverage she seeks, and starts to move again, but Bryan shakes his head, hands pressed to both of her hips to hold her steady. "Not yet," he says, standing up and turning to stand next to the table. Bree wraps her legs around his waist, enjoying the fullness of his cock inside of her, eager to see what comes next. Ryan stands up.

"You want more?" Bryan asks her again.

Bree nods, excitement filling her with anticipated pleasure. Ryan moves to stand facing his brother, and Bree feels Ryan's cock pressing against her ass. He slides closer as his brother pushes her backwards, and Bree is slowly filled with both cocks. The twins move slowly in tandem, the motion filling Bree with exquisite sensation.

"Fuck yes!" she cries, moving a little faster, letting herself take them both completely, pleasure scorching her entire body.

"Bree!" Bryan's commanding voice makes her look up at him, and he tilts his head to the side, where Bree realizes Josh has climbed up on the table and is now standing on it, his hard cock about level with her face. "Suck him!"

Bree obeys, relishing in the fullness of her body, the competing sensations building as the boys take her to another level. Bree comes just as Josh explodes, cum filling her mouth and running down her chin, and then the twins roar their own pleasure, and they all stand there for a long moment, lost in pure pleasure.

Slowly, Bree comes back to herself, letting Josh's cock slip out of her mouth. Ryan's cock slides out of her ass, and Bryan lifts her off him and sets her gently on the edge of the table. All three guys collapse on the table around her, everyone breathing hard.

"Well," Bree says, after a long moment where she catches her breath. "That gives a whole new meaning to cramming."

"I did so well on my midterm," Bree tells Josh. "I was hoping we could do something similar for finals."

Josh smiles at her as they walk across campus to the Stallions Sports Facility. "Definitely," Josh agrees, looking over his shoulder to where Ryan and Bryan walk behind them. "Don't you worry. We have something special planned."

"Oh?" Bree asks. "Like what?"

"If we told you, it wouldn't be a surprise," Ryan says.

"I hope you like it," Bryan adds, smiling shyly at her.

Bree returns the smile. "I'm sure I will." She grabs Josh's hand as they walk, addressing all three of them. "You guys were a huge help last time. I have an A in A&P right now."

"Great," Josh says. "And tonight, we're going to help you keep it."

They approach the sliding glass doors and walk inside, the cool air conditioned air hitting them with a blast. Bree follows Josh into the locker room, sitting down on one of the benches in front of the lockers. She has been to their training area many times since studying for midterms, so she is comfortable enough. She's met some of the guys on the rest of the team, so when they walk out from the showers to reach for their lockers, she greets them. None of them seem to mind a girl in the locker room; in fact, they seem to relish strutting around in their towels, flashing her whenever they get the chance.

Bree watches Aaron, the blonde quarterback, as he approaches, taking a moment to appreciate the sculpted muscles of his chest. To her disappointment, he isn't wearing a towel, just gym shorts, but his hair is a little wet, like he just came in from outside.

"Hey Aaron," she says. "How was practice?"

He shrugs, flashing her that perfect smile complete with dimples. "Practice was fine." He looks at Josh. "But I'm looking forward to the afterparty."

Bree raises an eyebrow. "What afterparty? I'm just here to study for finals."

He nods. "I know. I thought we'd get some of the guys to help out, make sure you really know everything you need to." He bites his lip.

Bree cocks her head at him, mind cycling through all manner of fantasies. "What did you have in mind?" she asks the quarterback, hoping he says what she's thinking. Sex with the team is a Bucket List item.

"Well," he says, gesturing at Ryan and Bryan sitting on either side of her, with Josh moving off to her right, "you already know how helpful these guys can be." He looks over his shoulder to the hallway leading out to the practice field. "You know," he suggests, "we could always add more players to the game." He pauses, then adds, "To assist in the... study session."

Bree bites her lip and considers the logistics. "Like how many more?"

Aaron smiles wide. "You already know these three, but how about Vince, Jason, and Corey?" As he says their names, three men walk into the room.

"Vince is our wide receiver," Aaron introduces, gesturing to a tall dark-skinned bald man with a beautiful face. Bree nods at him. She's had a few brief conversations with Vince while he and Josh study for chemistry. The thought of seeing him up close and personal is thrilling.

"Jason is our tight end," Aaron continues, pointing to a lean red-head with a shock of freckles across his pale face. Vince reaches over and smacks Jason on the ass.

"Tightest end in town," Vince says with a laugh.

"You know it," Jason tells him, turning so Bree can see the ass in question. It is a glorious ass, covered as it is in his gym shorts, and Bree nods. She wouldn't mind squeezing some of that ass.

"And you know Corey, our safety," Aaron finishes, nodding at the lean, caramel-skinned man standing on the end. Bree nods at him; she and Corey both had English together last semester.

"Hmm," Bree says, looking at the newcomers in turn. "It depends. How are you guys with body systems?"

"Solid," Vince offers, gesturing at his gorgeous abs. "My body is a perfect system."

"Apparently, I'm the ass man," Jason offers, "but this ass remembers enough to get by."

"I think you know I'm a team player," Corey reminds her. "We will get the job done."

Bree takes in the seven men in the room with her. She smirks. "Anyone else?" She looks around, noting the Billy the Bronco costume leaning in the corner, the purple and silver stallion mascot looking like it decided to take a break and sit down. Bree has the weird feeling that it is watching her, but she shrugs it off. There are enough eyes on her at the moment.

"Well…" Aaron begins.

Bree cocks her head. "What? Is there someone else you had in mind?"

He shrugs. "Phillipe is still outside practicing his kicks."

Bree pictures the beautiful kicker from Colombia, his dark hair, his bright eyes, his long limbs. She nods at Aaron, deciding to swing for the fences. "Sure." She's always wondered what it would be like to taste that mouth.

Aaron nods and Jason takes off, heading out to the back field. When he returns a few moments later with a sweaty but still gorgeous Phillipe, Bree stares at them all in turn: her team.

"So," Aaron says in the silence, "What do you think?"

"I think we should start with some ground rules," Josh offers, winking at her. "Bree is highly motivated by rewards and punishments." He looks at her. "I assume you have more flashcards?"

Bree nods, reaching down for her nearly forgotten bag and pulls out the worn stack of 3x5 cards. She holds them out, not sure who will be in charge of them. Aaron nods his head at the twins, and Ryan reaches out to grab them. "We'll switch off," he tells his brother.

"Let's see," Aaron says. "I think we should start with something easy." He looks at Ryan, who flips the top card and scans it, then shoves it into the middle of the stack and flips to the next one. He seems more pleased with this option.

"Forms the external body covering and protects deeper tissues from injury," he reads. "Contains cutaneous receptors and sweat glands."

Everyone looks at Bree, but she smirks at Josh, who winks at her. She remembers his touch on her skin as he whispered to her. "The integumentary system," she declares proudly.

Aaron nods. "A reward then. What would the lady prefer?"

Bree smiles broadly, a slow rush building in her lower belly. "Yes." She gives them all another once over, some of them still sweaty from practice. "And I think we should definitely start with a shower."

Aaron grins. "Good call." Bree lets the quarterback reach down, grab her slightly sweaty hand from her lap, and pull her gently to her feet. He leads her to the back right corner of the large room, the guys surrounding her in a circle as they walk by the massage tables and pass the two tubs—one filled with steaming water and the other with water Bree knows is icy cold. He pauses outside the open shower area, then slides his hands down to wrap around her waist. He leans down slowly, an offer, and when Bree turns her face up to his, he kisses her, mouth warm and lips soft against hers.

Hands run up her sides and a body presses against her back, a mouth kissing the back of her neck, and Bree recognizes Josh. His hands move slowly around to her front and slip down inside her sweatpants to press on her clit the way he knows she likes. She moans into Aaron's mouth, her hands reaching out and finding hard muscle. Aaron releases her mouth just as Josh's fingers begin to move in a slow sweet rhythm against her, and she leans back against him. Her hands abandon Aaaron and reach out to her sides, each encountering smooth skin over hard muscle—Corey and Vince on either side of her.

They respond by sliding the straps of her tank top down her arms, taking their time, reaching under each breast to lift it out of the cami. Bree is glad that she chose not to wear a bra tonight as the straps clear her hand. Together, they push the rest of the tank top down around her stomach, freeing her breasts completely. Hands cup her, fingers gently squeezing her nipples, and combined with Josh's constant rhythm between her legs, Bree comes suddenly, falling back into the cornerback.

He catches her easily, and Aaron releases her mouth, stepping back. Ryan and Bryan step forward and lift each of her legs, letting Corey and Vince slide both her sweatpants and her tank top down, leaving her naked. She shivers, and then she is being carried into the shower where the water is already pouring down from six showerheads, the three stalls on each side divided by a low half wall that juts out about two feet. The center of the shower is open, but still has three rain showerheads which pour water in a flow almost hard enough to massage muscles.

Corey and Vince stand on either side of her as she tilts her head back, letting the flow of the water soak her hair and rinse her face.

"I think it's time for another question," Aaron announces.

"Supports and protects the body's organs and provides the framework for muscles," Bryan reads quickly.

"Skeletal system," Bree tells them proudly, hands sliding from her hair down her body and settling on her hips. She pulls her face out of the stream and looks at them. She meets Jason's eyes and jerks her head at him to stand in front of her. The redhead obliges, sliding his shorts off in an instant and moving into the shower. Bree is pleased to see he has a long, lovely cock standing proudly in a thatch of red hair. She reaches for him, grabbing that cock first, and tugs him closer to her, letting the water flatten his hair to his head. She leans into the flow, hand slowly stroking his cock, and kisses him. Her other hand reaches out to the side, and then Corey's hands are touching hers. She drags his hand to her breast and leaves it there. Vince is quick to get the message, both leaning in to cup her full breasts. She is close to Jason, kissing him, but then she pulls away, and in the moment there is space between her and Jason, Corey and Vince lean in and begin to suck her nipples.

Bree moans, but doesn't lose her grip on Jason's cock, continuing to stroke him. A body moves behind her, and gentle hands caress her sides, and someone is kissing her neck. A hard cock presses against her ass. She turns to find Phillipe and kisses him, head turned to the left, while Corey and Vince continue to suck her nipples. Phillipe is an amazing kisser, and Bree loses herself in the feeling, barely noticing when Corey and Vince seem to shift a little. She does notice when Jason's cock moves out of reach of her hand, and he grabs her hand and moves it off to her right, where she can continue to stroke him where he stands between Vince and Phillipe. Her left hand is suddenly touching another hard cock, and she opens her eyes for a second to find Josh on her left. She grabs the cock and begins stroking in rhythm with Jason and returns to kissing Phillipe.

New hands are suddenly on both of her hips, tugging her forward slightly, and a warm mouth sucks her clit, tongue licking her gently and sucking hard again. She moans, legs going weak at the spike of sensation, and the men support her weight easily. Her nipples contract, pleasure spiraling up from her middle, and she comes hard against the mouth. Through the haze of her delight, she looks down her body to see the blonde hair of Aaron's head between her legs. He looks up at her and winks, then sucks hard again, this time sliding two fingers inside of her. Bree bucks wildly against him, coming again, and she goes boneless for a moment.

Phillipe stops kissing her, and hands hold her steady, but Aaron's mouth leaves her sensitive skin for a moment, giving her a break. Then hands are rubbing shampoo into her hair, and others hands are sliding soap along her skin, and she stands there, regaining the solidity in her legs, letting the men wash her like a queen.

When she is completely rinsed, Aaron stands up and says, "I think it's time for another question."

Ryan and Bryan are standing just outside the shower, watching the festivities but not joining in, though each has his cock out and is slowly stroking it. Bree smiles at each in turn, knowing she will have her way with them too, in time.

Ryan lets go of his cock and reaches for the stack of cards resting on the ledge behind him. He flips to the next one, grins, and reads, "Houses white blood cells involved in immunity."

Bree sighs, reveling in the loose feel of her body under the warm water. "I feel pretty immune right now," she moans.

"What's the system?" Bryan asks. "Name it."

"I know it," Bree stalls, trying to get her brain to focus.

"Then tell us," Aaron says, giving her ass a quick swat.

Bree squeaks. "It's the..." Her voice trails off, her brain spinning.

Aaron reaches behind him and shuts off the water, and Bree is standing there, naked and dripping. "I think it might be time for a punishment, boys."

Bree giggles. "I think my punishment should definitely be a cock in the mouth," she suggests, sinking to her knees.

"That's a reward, Bree," Josh says. "You know the rules."

Bree frowns, then thinks again. "Immunity..." Hands reach out to caress her shoulders gently, sliding on her wet skin from the outside of her upper arm and back up to the sides of her neck. "Think, my beauty," Phillipe croons behind her, and the answer hits her. "Lymphatic system!"

"Nice," Aaron tells her. "Now you get a reward." He looks around. "Who would you like?"

Bree scans the eager faces and turns to look at Phillipe behind her. "I think I'll start here," she says, and leans forward to take his cock into her mouth. She takes two slow pulls, then gestures with each hand. Corey and Vince step up immediately, and she is rewarded with a cock in each hand. Aaron kneels behind her, his cock pressing into her back, and he leans down to kiss her neck. She opens her eyes to glance to her right, meeting Josh's eyes as she sucks Phillipe's cock. She turns her head, locking eyes with Jason next, and when she finally turns her gaze up to watch Phillipe's face, the kicker lets loose with a long stream of Spanish before exploding in her mouth. Bree giggles, lets go of Vince and Corey, and stands up, kissing Phillipe hard, cum rolling down her chin. Aaron groans, and then he is standing up behind her, hard cock pressed against her entrance.

"You want this cock?" he asks, and Bree releases Phillipe's mouth long enough to say yes, pushing back against him, eager to feel him inside of her. He slides inside easily, filling her, and she groans, finding Phillipe's mouth again. Her hands reach out to either side, and Corey and Vince are where she left them. She strokes them both as Aaron pumps into her, and soon she is shuddering her release, moaning into Phillipe's mouth as she sinks against him.

Aaron leans back, tugging her backwards, and then he is sitting on the floor, and she is on top of him, her back to his chest. He lifts her gently, letting her slide up and down a few times as he adjusts her legs to spread them wide on either side of his own. Bree moves her feet, attempting to shift into reverse cowgirl position, but he holds her steady. "Oh no," he tells her, trailing kisses along her neck. "Stay like that."

Jason moves between her legs, and Bree reaches out for that long cock, but he leans down instead, face between her thighs, his tongue quick and adept, and soon Bree is coming again, hands pressed against the back of his head. Her heart is still pounding when Aaron gently lifts her off his cock, and then puts his cock against her asshole.

"You ready for this?" he asks.

"Maybe," she replies, "but I want Jason in my ass." She turns around to face him, pressing against his chest until he lays down on the shower floor. She climbs on, relishing the feel of him inside of her again and leans forward. "Josh," she says, gesturing toward him. "Bring me that cock." The cornerback obliges, standing in front of her, a foot on either side of Aaron's head.

Jason scoots in behind her, hands pressing against her ass. Corey and Vince move to either side, lifting her up and down in a gentle rhythm as Jason slides first one and then two fingers into her ass. "Oh yes!" she moans, leaning forward to take Josh into her mouth. She comes hard, the orgasm shaking her, and while she is still recovering, Jason replaces his fingers with his cock, and the thin length slips inside of her. She grunts, and then Bree is aware of nothing but pleasure as both cocks move inside of her. Hands cup her breast, another hand slides down to press against her clit and begins to rub. The sensations quickly overwhelm her, and as she clenches in her orgasm, she feels Aaron let go inside of him. A moment later Jason is also cumming. Josh is the last to let go, and Bree leans back without thinking, cum running down her chin. Vince and Corey lift her away, and someone turns on the shower again.

Hands rub her down, soaping her slowly and gently, and Bree isn't paying attention to who is attached to what anymore. A mouth finds her clit in the warm water, and she sags backwards into another body, who cups her under the arms to hold her upright.

"More?" a voice says, and Bree nods, then finds her voice.

"Yes," she tells them. "I'm not done yet. More."

The shower turns off, and hands carry her out, a soft towel rubbing against her skin. She is laid down somewhere, and Bree opens her eyes to recognize the massage table. Her team surrounds her, and she smiles at them all.

"What now?" Aaron asks.

Bree considers. She looks at Corey and Vince in turn. "I feel like you guys deserve some one on one time," she says, crawling up on her hands and knees between them.

Corey takes the hint, scooting up behind her and resting the tip of his cock against her opening. Vince moves to kneel in front of her, cock even with her mouth. She sucks in at the same moment she presses back against Corey, the cock sliding inside of her, ultra-sensitive skin singing in response to the stimulation. "God," she moans against Vince's cock, moving back and forth in a gentle, mind-blowing rhythm. She abandons the cock in her mouth, grabbing him with her hand instead focusing on Corey and that glorious orgasm building again inside of her. "Fuck!" she yells, squeezing Vince's cock and pressing hard against Corey. "Fuck me!" And then Corey is pounding her, gentleness forgotten, sensitive skin forgotten, and Bree comes again, a scream tearing from her throat. Corey comes hard against her, and she lays there for a moment to collect herself, Vince's cock forgotten in her head.

After a long moment, she looks up at him. "Oh no!" She takes a deep breath. "Come on, Vince," she says. "Your turn."

Vince flips her onto her back, and tugs her toward him, sheathing himself to the core in one motion, setting a fast rhythm as if he knows she doesn't have much left in her. She wraps her legs around his hips, hands gripping his ass, urging him on with grunts and moans. She comes again when he does, and they lay together, sticky with sweat and pleasure. Vince gets up after a moment and falls beside her. Bree lays on her back, breathing hard. Gentle hards stroke her skin, but only to touch, not to come. Her body relaxes, coming down from the intense pleasure, and after a moment, she opens her eyes and leans up on her elbows.

She looks at where the twins are sitting on the edge of the table. "I believe it's your turn," she says. "You definitely deserve something for being such good study partners."

"Speaking of studying," Aaron offers, "I think it's time for another question."

Bree sighs, but leans back. "Hit me," she tells them, trying to get her brain back in study mode.

Bryan stands up to retrieve the cards from where he left them on the edge of the shower. Walking back, he reads the top one, "Pumps blood to deliver nutrients to major organs."

Bree snickers. "Cardiovascular system. I certainly worked mine out tonight."

The twins nod in unison and move closer to her. Bryan grabs her legs and drags her down to the edge of the table. Her legs bend at the knees and her feet land flat on the floor. Bree is short, and table is very low.

"Wait," Aaron says. There is a low clicking sound, and Bree feels the bed being raised beneath her. Aaron raises it until her feet dangle, and Bryan tugs her the rest of the way to the edge, standing between her legs with his cock pressed against her. Ryan climbs up on her right and kneels next to her. He gives her a quizzical look, head cocked.

"What?" Bree asks.

"Can I fuck those perfect titties?" he asks.

Bree looks down at her chest. "Sure," she says. "Get over here with that huge cock."

Ryan climbs on top of her, sitting on her stomach and sliding his cock between the valley of her breasts. Bree presses them together around him, and Ryan sighs with pleasure. As Ryan begins to move, Bryan slides gently inside her, moving slowly against her battered skin, hands gripping her hips.

Bree closes her eyes again, losing herself in the moment, aware of the eyes of the team on her. She opens her eyes and looks at each of them in turn. "Come on me," she offers. Aaron and Phillipe start to move, but the sound of a voice makes everyone freeze in place.

"And what is happening here?" a lush female voice demands. "I don't recall giving anyone permission to come all over anyone."

Bree turns to stare at the newcomer, a small red-haired woman wearing a white tank top with the Stallions logo and a short purple pleated skirt.

"Coach!" Aaron says. "We didn't think you were still here!"

"Clearly," Coach Smith says, giving the twins a glare. "Did I say you could stop?"

Bryan resumes his motion and Ryan slowly grinds into Bree's breasts while Bree stares at the coach incredulously. "Umm," she stammers. "They are helping me study?"

Coach Smith nods. "I see. And how is it going?"

Bree grins stupidly. "Amazingly," she admits, Bryan's cock hitting that perfect stride inside of her, a low glow building in her belly again, even with the Coach watching. "They are wonderful partners."

"Tell me something I don't know," Coach Smith says. "But how are you?" She gives Bree a long look. "Are you worthy of my boys?"

Bree looks around at the satisfied faces around her. "I think I'm doing just fine," she declares, hooking her legs around Bryan's hips and urging him faster, meeting the coach's eyes and he moves faster in her, hands pressing hard on her breasts as Ryan rocks back and forth, his cock slipping against her skin.

"Let's see," Coach Smith declares, and then she is climbing onto the table, putting one leg on either side of Bree's head, and she squats right on Bree's face, bringing her bare pussy to Bree's open mouth. Bree is so shocked that for a moment she can do nothing, but her hands reach up automatically to cup Coach's perfect ass beneath the skirt, and then she is moving her mouth, marveling at the taste of pussy against her lips, her tongue slipping out to find her clit. The woman bounces on Bree's face, and Bree licks again, her tongue finding a hard bump and sucking it into her mouth.

"Oh yes!" Coach Smith yells. "You are good!" She rocks her hips against Bree's face, and Bree sucks some more, the fingers of one hand sliding a little so she can slide a finger inside Coach's pussy.

"Fuck those titties, Ryan," Coach barks. "I want to see cum everywhere." There is a sound like kissing, and Bree wonders if

Coach is kissing Ryan, but then Coach commands, "Fuck that pussy like you mean it, Bryan!"

Bryan obeys, pumping into Bree, and she clutches him with her legs, the orgasm spiraling up hard and fast. "And you," Coach Smith orders, "suck my pussy! I want to come all over that lovely face!" Bree shoves her fingers inside Coach's pussy the way she likes in her own pleasure, mouth sucking hard on her clit, and then the wave hits her and she is shuddering against Bryan as he cums, Ryan's cum floods over her breasts, and Coach Smith trembles against her face with a cry. More warmth hits Bree's skin from other angles, hot liquid running down her skin.

Coach Smith leaps off Bree's face in a display of casual athleticism, and stands there, taking them all in. Ryan and Bryan are breathing hard. Bree's heart is still pounding. The team is kneeling around them on the table, dicks still in their hands.

"I hope my boys did you proud tonight," Coach announces. "And good luck on that final exam." She turns and walks out of the room, disappearing down the hallway. A heavy door shuts behind her.

Bree lays there on the table, still catching her breath and licking her lips, the taste of Coach still in her mouth. Ryan leans forward and kisses her slowly, sensually. He releases her, and climbs off her stomach, and Bryan leans down to kiss her as well. He pulls back after a moment, slipping out of her, and then Phillipe is leaning down to kiss her too, followed by slow kisses from Corey, Vince, Jason, and Aaron. Josh waits until the end, then settles in next to her head and kisses her long and passionately.

Bree sits up slowly, body languid and sticky with spent pleasure.

"So," Aaron asks her, "you think you're ready for that final now?"

Bree smiles at him. "Best. Studygroup. Ever."

ALI WHIPPE

li Whippe is the pen name of a professor in the higher education system who delights in imagining naughty distractions while enduring endless mind-numbing committee meetings. She loves to push the boundaries of the written word and the imagination, knowing that life at work would be way more exciting if more people didn't wear panties.

Fantasy/Paranormal Romance

Valerie Willis
Cedric the Demonic Knight
Romasanta: Father of Werewolves
The Oracle: Keeper of the Gaea's Gate
Artemis: Eye of Gaea
King Incubus: A New Reign

J.M. Paquette
Klauden's Ring
Solyn's Body
Hannah's Heart

4HorsemenPublications.com